The C_
of the
Full Moon

Written by
Stephanie Baudet

Illustrated by David Stansfield

First Published
January 05 in Great Britain by

PUBLISHING

ISBN-10: 1-904904-11-4
ISBN-13: 978-1-904904-11-3

Educational Printing Services Limited
Albion Mill, Water Street, Great Harwood, Blackburn BB6 7QR
Telephone: (01254) 882080   Fax: (01254) 882010
E-mail: enquiries@eprint.co.uk   Website: www.eprint.co.uk

Contents

Chapter 1
The Green Ghost

I ran, slipping and stumbling on twigs and rotting leaves. Bushes clutched at my clothes and scratched my arms. I dare not look round. All I could hear was the rasping of my breath and a pulse thudding somewhere in my head.

The trees were thinning out. I put on an extra effort and came out of the woods, swung round the end house and flung open our back gate. It crashed shut and made Mum jump. She was sitting in the garden reading the paper.

'Simon! Are you all right?'

I couldn't speak I was so out of breath. Sweat was running in my eyes and I brushed my hand across my forehead.

'Something has frightened you,' said Mum. She looked at me closely. 'What was it?'

I felt a bit calmer. 'Oh, nothing, Mum. Just someone in the woods. Made me jump, that's all.' I knew I had to make light of it.

Mum worried.

'What did he say? Was he chasing you? Tell me, Simon!'

'No Mum. It was nothing. He just appeared, that's all. I didn't hear him coming so it gave me a fright. He was dressed all in green like some daft wally playing Robin Hood.'

'I don't like you playing all alone in the woods, Simon.'

'I wasn't. Mick was with me but he went home for lunch. I'd just stopped at the spring for a drink but that water's warm. Then this bloke appeared. He was all right. Honest, Mum.'

But what I didn't tell Mum was the scariest thing of all.

The man had no face! Where his head should have been there was only a misty grey round shape.

Then he just disappeared.

She was still frowning at me. Any minute now she'd forbid me from going into the woods.

'I'm hungry,' I said quickly.

Mum pressed a hand to her forehead. 'Do you mind getting your own lunch, love?' She folded up the newspaper and sighed.

'I've got an awful headache again. I think I'll go and lie down for half an hour.'

Mum was always getting headaches lately. I hoped it was nothing bad. I put together a cheese and tomato sandwich. Mick should have finished his lunch by now and I couldn't wait to tell him what I'd seen.

Mick grinned, his teeth very white in his freckled face. 'Are you telling me you saw a ghost? In the daytime?'

'Real people don't just appear and disappear. You can always hear them coming in the woods with all the dead leaves and twigs.'

'Come on, show me then,' said Mick. 'We'll go to the spring and see if he appears again. Why didn't you take a photo of him? You said you want to be a reporter.'

I wished I had but I'd been too scared at the time. And you couldn't just snap people close up without saying anything.

'I don't care if you believe me or not.'

'Course you do.'

Usually I liked being in the woods. It smelt fresh and clean. Sometimes I saw a rabbit or a pheasant.

We got to the spring.

'I don't see any green man,' said Mick. He smirked.

I said nothing. I sat down on the bank and watched the clear water bubbling up between the roots of the oak.

'Leave it, Mick.'

Mick sat down too. 'I'm thirsty. Can you drink this water?'

'Yeah, but it's warm.'

Mick splashed some on his face. 'Did I tell you Dad's bought me a new football? Real leather. We're going to try it out on the common tonight.'

I threw a pebble into the pool and watched the ripples spread out.

'I'll be famous one day,' went on Mick. 'Mick Farley, England's greatest footballer. You can come and interview me.'

I grinned at him. 'You'd better give me your autograph now. Then I can sell it for a thousand pounds when you're famous!'

Mick's laugh rang out.

So what if he didn't believe me about the green man? I was beginning to think it had been a trick of the light. It's a good thing Mick hadn't seen me run away!

'There he is,' said Mick, 'but he's not dressed in green.'

There were two men, doing some sort of measuring.

'That's not him,' I said. 'What are they doing?'

'Surveying,' said Mick in his know-it-all voice.

'What's that?'

'You know. Measuring up land before they build something.'

'Not here. They'd have to chop down lots of trees. How do you know that's what they're doing?'

Mick pulled a face. 'My Dad's a builder, remember?'

'But they can't build here, Mick.'

That evening I found out I was wrong. Dad came in holding the local newspaper and looking very angry.

'They can't do this!' he exploded, and shook the paper crossly. 'Cut down some of the woods to build on. It's criminal!'

'We saw them surveying today,' I said.

Mum took the paper and began reading it. She screwed up her eyes a little.

'What's wrong with your eyes, Mum?'

Mum glared at me. 'Nothing,' she snapped. 'I just had a headache earlier, as you know.'

'We've got to do something!' said Dad.

Mum spun round to face him. 'About my headaches?'

'About the building,' said Dad.

'We can start a petition,' said Mum.

'Will it change their minds if we get a lot of people to sign?' I asked.

'It might,' said Mum.

'It won't!' said Dad.

'I'll take the petition to school,' I said.

None of the kids would want the woods to be destroyed to build more houses. I was certain of that.

Chapter 2
Opposite Sides

I asked Mick to sign it first. He took the pen and read the article.

'No way!' He shoved them back at me. 'My Dad's got that contract. He's doing the building.'

I looked at him in amazement. 'You didn't tell me yesterday!'

'I didn't know then.'

'He can't cut down the woods!'

'It's only part of the woods. They need more houses and shops.'

Then he said in a loud voice so that everyone could hear: 'They are building a sports centre too.' He kicked at an imaginary football.

I looked at the article again. 'There's not going to be a football field. It says a building for gym and table tennis.'

'But there might be weights! Yeah!' He flexed his arms.

I wasn't interested. Trees were going to be cut down. Trees that had taken years to grow. Not only that, but much wildlife would be made homeless too. All for a sports centre and more houses and shops.

Mick and I used to be best friends and now we were acting like enemies. First he had laughed at me about the green man and now we were on opposite sides about the building.

I walked home through the town to avoid Mick. I went to the library too. There was a display board with photos and newspaper cuttings pinned to it.

LOCAL FOLKLORE was printed across the top. I looked at it as I waited to renew my book.

Two words jumped out at me. Green man. I looked closer.

Over the years people had seen a faceless green figure in the forest . . . and there was a holy well there too.

When it was my turn I said: 'How can I get a copy of that, please?'

'I'll do you a photocopy, love,' said the librarian. 'Ten pence.'

I couldn't wait to get home and read the article properly.

Chapter 3
The Demonstration

The green man ghost had been seen many times before over the centuries. Legend had it that he was the Spirit of the Forest, the protector of the trees and all life within. He was supposed to have put a curse on whoever cut down the trees.

Whoever dares destroy these trees
Or harms a creature in their care
At full moon shall he meet his doom
And all who follow him, beware!

A lot of the forest had been cut down over the centuries. The oak had been used for building ships in the seventeenth and eighteenth centuries. No-one knew if the curse had come true. Perhaps the ships had sunk in battle.

I read the rhyming curse again. Was it true? Would something bad happen to anyone who cut down the trees? Something occurred to me. It was Mick's Dad, wasn't it? He was the builder. He was in charge of cutting down the trees. I must go and tell Mick so that he could warn his father.

Then I remembered that Mick and I weren't friends at the moment. Mick would only laugh anyway. Probably his Dad would too. People didn't believe in curses nowadays

I read the rest of the article.

The green man ghost was most often seen near the holy well, or spring, in the north east corner of the wood.

The spring! That was where I'd seen it! Since the fourteenth century people had gone to the spring to drink its healing waters. It was very good for eye ailments. The custom was to leave money in return for the water.

Perhaps it would cure Mum's eyes.

I found an empty drink bottle to fill with spring water and went out. Two mechanical diggers were already in place at the edge of the woods.

The slope beside the little stream was really steep. When I reached the spring I tried not to think of what I'd seen yesterday.

I filled the bottle and then took a five pence piece out of my pocket and threw it into the pool. It sank to the bottom and lay glinting in the clear water.

There was a rustling noise and my heart missed a beat.

Mick stood by the oak, grinning. 'Sorry I haven't got my green outfit on today.'

I tried to grin back. Should I tell him about the curse . . . but how could I?

Mick saw the coin at the bottom of the pool. 'Hey! There's 5p!' He pushed up his sleeve and got down onto his stomach, leaning out over the edge of the water.

'Leave it!' I yelled.

'Why?' Mick saw the bottle of water. 'What's that for?'

'It's healing water for my Mum's eyes.'

'You must be daft!' scoffed Mick. 'Did you chuck that 5p in? Water's free.' He plunged in his hand and grasped the coin.

I got up and walked away. Tears of anger stung my eyes.

I hate Mick Farley!

Back at the building site an ambulance was just moving slowly over the bumpy ground.

'You keep away from here!' shouted one of the workmen, waving his arms. 'This machinery is dangerous!'

'What happened?' I asked.

'Never you mind! Just clear off, do you hear?'

It was Mum who told me.

'A shovel came loose and fell,' she said.

'One of the big shovels on the digger. It crushed the foot of one of the workmen. Lucky he wasn't killed.'

It's started, I thought. The curse has started working.

'Serves 'em right,' Dad said, unkindly. 'I've got plenty of support. We're meeting at seven o'clock tomorrow evening and staging a demonstration. We've invited the local press to attend.'

'Can I go?' I asked.

'No,' said Mum, quickly.

'Oh Mum . . . '

'Why not,' said Dad, 'let the boy fight for his beliefs.'

I'd seen demonstrations on TV. They did look a bit scary and often got violent but this was going to be a peaceful one. People carrying banners. It was sure to work. If Mick's Dad saw that so many people didn't want more houses and shops he wouldn't build them, would he?

More people than I ever imagined met at the edge of the woods the next evening. Already quite a few trees had been cut down. Many people carried banners which said things like:
'LEAVE OUR WOODS ALONE' and 'NO MORE HOUSES'.

A car drove up and two men from the council got out.

The crowd jeered and those with banners began to wave them and surge onto the building site. The men stood and stared, uncertain what to do.

'Save our woods!' shouted a voice and the crowd took up the chant, louder and louder as more and more people joined in.

I felt myself being pushed and jostled and then my feet were knocked from under me and I crashed to the ground. Every time I tried to get up people kicked me as they struggled to get away. For the first time I felt panic.

I knew that people had been trampled to death this way.

'You all right, son?' With relief I saw Dad's white face looming over me and then his firm grasp hauled me to my feet.

'Yes, Dad.' My voice didn't seem to belong to me. I felt dizzy and sick.

The crowd had scattered.

'I got shoved by one of those hooligans and then I lost sight of you,' said Dad. 'Troublemakers! The police are on their way.' I felt his hand on my shoulder. 'Come on, son. Let's get you home.'

'That wasn't a very peaceful demonstration was it, Dad?' My voice shook and I couldn't seem to do anything about it.

Dad looked suddenly furious. 'It was until that bunch of yobs arrived,' he said through clenched teeth. 'Now, we've no chance.'

Chapter 4
Trapped!

That night I dreamt of gangs of yobs running through the woods chased by mechanical diggers and a green ghost sitting in a tree watching.

In the morning I got out of bed and went to the window. The woods were quiet now but I couldn't get last night out of my mind.

One of the diggers was lying on its side! I could see one of its big rear wheels in the air.

The yobs must have been back!

I threw on some clothes and went out. The woods were noisy with bird song as I went across to where the diggers were. Both of them had been moved. I remembered that the bigger one had been against a tree as if ready to push it down. Now it was out of the woods and right up against the wall of someone's garden.

The other digger had been driven half into the stream running down from the spring. One of its back wheels had gone down the bank and the whole thing tipped on its side.

Why had the vandals done this? First they had frightened the people at the demonstration and now they had moved and tipped over the diggers.

It didn't make sense.

A movement in the trees made me look up. Were they still here, hiding in the woods?

A slight breeze rustled the leaves and I screwed up my eyes and peered into the dim depths of the woods.

Then I saw the tall green figure, clear and solid in every way except for the grey hazy oval where his face should be.

Yes!

It was true! It was real!

I started walking towards it.

The figure slowly faded.

By the time I reached the spot where it had stood there was nothing except an icy cold pocket of air. I shivered and moved off up the slope towards the spring. The air was warm again.

The sun filtered through the leaves and splashed brilliant patches of dancing light onto the ground.

I needed more water for Mum so I filled the bottle again. I'd be late for school if I didn't get a move on.

The workmen had arrived at the building site and were staring crossly at the upturned digger. Then a police car arrived and two policemen got out. One of them saw me and came over.

'Do you live near here, son?'

'Just there,' I pointed.

'Did you see or hear anything last night? People hanging around here or engines running?'

'No.'

The policeman strode off. I wondered whether the police suspected the demonstrators or the yobs. But they were wrong. Something else was stopping the workmen from cutting down the trees. I was sure of it now.

'Mick's staying tonight,' said Mum at breakfast.

My heart sank.

'I thought you'd be pleased,' she said, seeing my face. 'He is your best friend, isn't he?'

'Not now.'

Mum tutted and shook her head. 'I'm sorry, Simon, but his parents are going out for the evening and won't be back until late. It was arranged ages ago.'

The whole evening and night in the same room as Mick Farley! How could Mum do this?

'Couldn't he stay with one of his other friends?'

'He's staying here!' shouted Mum. 'And that's the end of it!'

I left for school in a miserable mood.

The evening with Mick didn't turn out as bad as I'd thought it would be. We never once talked about the green man or the new buildings. He'd brought a video and we watched that and had a good laugh like we used to when we were real mates.

Later in bed and under cover of the darkness I tried to tell him about the curse.

'Mick.'

'Yeah?'

'Do you believe in curses?'

'What do you mean?'

'You know,' I said, 'when somebody puts a curse on something and says that bad things will happen to anyone who touches it. Things like that.'

'You mean like witches?'

'Sort of.'

'Dunno. Maybe people do have powers like that.'

I took a deep breath. 'There's a curse on the woods,' I said.

Mick snorted. 'Not that again!'

'Well, I was only thinking of your Dad.'

'You are daft, Simon. You believe anything. My Dad can look after himself, curse or no curse.'

I heard him turn over and snuggle into the bedclothes. Well, I'd done my best. I couldn't help it if no-one would listen.

Something woke me in the night. I could see a full moon through a gap in the curtains and I stared at it for a few seconds.

Something stirred in my brain. *'At full moon shall he meet his doom.'*

I shivered and snuggled further into the bed but a noise aroused me again. A rumbling sound.

I raised my head to hear more clearly. Then I flung back the bedclothes and got out of bed.

'What's the matter?' asked Mick, sleepily.

'The diggers are moving again,' I whispered, 'I'm going out to see.' I started pulling my jeans over my pyjamas.

Mick got up quickly. 'We'd better call Dad,' he said. 'He was really mad yesterday. They had to call in a crane to pull up that tipped over digger.'

'I'm going to see first!' I had to find out the truth although I knew it already.

'Don't be daft! Those yobs will be right pleased if we turn up to watch them.'

'It's not them. Come and see.' I wasn't afraid now. Only excited.

We crept downstairs and out of the back door. At the edge of the site we stopped.

'We ought to phone Dad,' said Mick again.

The large digger was rumbling towards the steep slope where the stream from the spring flowed down.

Its large shovel was lifted high in the air.

Suddenly there was a frantic movement in front of it.

'It's a deer, I think,' I said. 'It's trapped.'

We ran forward. The deer's leg was caught in some barbed wire. It was pulling frantically, tearing the flesh of its leg. A trickle of blood ran down its smooth fur and dripped onto the ground.

'You hold him,' I said. 'I'll get his leg free. Quick!'

The digger moved closer like a great lumbering orange monster.

The deer ran off and it was then that we realised that it was too late to escape. The digger was almost on us, and just as the great shovel rode over our heads and ploughed into the hard earth of the slope we dived into a hollow in the bank.

The caterpillar wheels slid round on the spot for a few seconds and then the engine died. The great machine shuddered to a standstill two metres from us.

There was silence. The smaller digger must have stopped too. Mick's hand gripped my arm.

'Did you see?' he whispered shakily. 'There was no driver!'

'I know.'

We were trapped. The machine was pinning us against the hillside. We searched for a gap big enough to escape through but there were none.

'Do you think we ought to call for help?' asked Mick.

'It's no use.'

'Why not? Those boys might still be around. I don't think they meant to trap us.'

I sighed with exasperation. 'I told you. It wasn't them.'

'Who was it then?'

I told Mick about the green man. About the Spirit of the Forest and the curse. He didn't laugh this time.

'It's a full moon tonight,' he said. 'But why should the green man try to kill us?'

'He didn't. He just wants to disrupt the workmen. To stop the work.'

'What are we going to do?' wailed Mick. 'We should have brought a mobile.'

I peered out through a gap. It seemed to have got darker. The moon was still visible but dark clouds were gathering too. It looked like rain. I turned back to Mick.

'We'd better just try to keep warm and dry for the night,' I said. 'When we hear the workmen arrive we'll yell like mad. Once they start up the diggers they'll never hear us.'

Chapter 5
Rising Tides

Mick was silent for a moment and then he laughed harshly. 'You almost had me for a minute there, Si. Green man! I'll believe it when I see it.'

I said nothing but pressed the light button on my watch. Two-ten. It was going to be a long night.

A fox looked in on us once, its sharp nose poked through the small gap between the caterpillar wheels and the bank.

Its brown eyes stared into mine for a second or two, glinting in the moonlight, and then it was gone.

It grew colder. Dark clouds rolled over the moon, blotting out the light. I thought of my warm bed and wished I'd never left it.

Mick had been right. We should just have called his Dad. We were trapped and we hadn't proved anything. Perhaps it had been the yobs after all.

Rain began to ping onto the shovel above our heads. Soon it was a thundering roar and there were flashes of lightning.

'What if Dad and the other men don't come today,' said Mick. 'They can't work if it's too wet.'

I hadn't thought of that.

The shovel above our heads kept us fairly dry but the ground became soggy.

'Listen to the stream,' shouted Mick.

I nodded in the darkness. 'It sounds more like a raging river.'

'Do you think the pool is overflowing?'

There was certainly a lot of water rushing down the hillside now. Where was it all coming from? With a shock, I remembered something I'd read recently about underground water. The tides of the oceans were affected by the moon and so were underground lakes and rivers. They were at their highest level at full moon.

That was tonight! And not only that, it had been raining heavily for a couple of hours now.

Mick must have sensed something because he said: 'What's wrong?'

I had to tell him. This wasn't legend. It was fact.

His mind worked quickly. 'All that water rising up underground, coming out of the spring and then pouring down the hillside. It could cause flooding . . . and landslides.'

'And we're trapped here,' I said.

It was a terrifying thought. Tons of mud sliding down on top of us, burying us. No-one knew we were here. The workmen certainly couldn't work in this weather.

Dawn came at last, grey and miserable. The rain stopped.

We were sitting in several centimetres of water and couldn't stop shivering.

'It's a quarter to eight,' I said at last.
'Get ready to start shouting - in case the
workmen come.'

I didn't hold out much hope. Through the
small gap I could just see the track the
workmen would use.

Eight o'clock came and went. One or two cars passed along the main road but none stopped.

At twenty past eight a car did stop and two men got out and stared across in our direction.

'Shout!' I yelled.

'HELP!'

The men didn't hear. I thought I could hear the car engine running.

'HELP!' we yelled again.

The two men got back into the car and drove off.

'Why don't we wave something through the gap,' suggested Mick.

'Good thinking, Mick!' I cheered up a little. 'I've got a white T-shirt on.' I stripped it off from under my anorak and pushed it through the gap.

'Get ready to wave it like mad when any car passes along the road,' said Mick.

Ten minutes later a car did come along - and stopped. A man got out.

'It's Dad!' gasped Mick.

The rain had started again and pounded on the shovel.

'Dad!' we yelled, with me frantically waving my shirt.

A face appeared in the gap. 'Mick! Simon! What on earth are you two doing here?'

He looked up above the machine at the hillside, a worried expression on his face.

'I've got to get you out. I heard the machines had been moved again and came over to have a look. We can't work in this weather.'

He disappeared and a few minutes later we heard the door of the cab slam and the engine of the big digger start up.

The caterpillar wheels began to turn slowly, splattering mud all over us. Gradually the great machine backed away. As soon as the gap was wide enough we climbed out.

I felt stiff from being crouched up for so long and our clothes clung to us. My feet squelched inside my sodden trainers.

We started back towards my house but there was a rending tearing noise behind us. We turned and watched in horror as a huge tree growing part way up the hillside started to topple.

'Dad!' screamed Mick.

It was like watching a film in slow motion. The tree crashed down, torn up by the roots. Its thick foliage completely covered the digger. At the same time a whole section of the hillside began to move, bringing smaller trees with it. It slid in one huge jumbled mass of mud, rocks and trees and completely engulfed the big digger, with Mick's Dad inside.

Chapter 6
The Curse

Mick started running towards the digger.

I ran after him and grabbed his sleeve. 'You can't do anything, Mick. We've got to get help.'

We burst in through the back door of my house, startling Mum.

'Simon! . . . you're soaking wet . . .'

'Mick's Dad,' I gasped, trying to get my breath. 'He's trapped in the digger and there's been a landslide.'

Mum didn't hesitate. She ran into the hall to phone 999.

'Upstairs and get changed, both of you,' she said, punching in the numbers. 'I'll phone your Mum, Mick.'

Neither of us spoke while we changed. I found my camera in my wet anorak pocket and dried it with a towel, hoping it would be all right.

By the time we got outside again the rescue services were hard at work. With the small digger they were removing mud and earth from around the larger one. When the big fallen tree emerged they attached a cable to the trunk and began hauling, the great tractor wheels of the digger slipping a little on the wet ground.

Finally the thick tread gripped and slowly the tree shifted, bringing mud and rocks with it.

Mick's Mum stood with us, watching, an arm round her son's shoulders. None of us knew what to expect. It was as if the world had stopped.

At last the cab of the digger was clear and the ambulance men wheeled their stretcher with difficulty and squelched over the sodden ground in their clean black shoes.

Mick's Dad was lifted out onto the stretcher. He wasn't moving. Mrs Farley gave a sort of choked cry. I was thinking about the curse. *'At full moon shall he meet his doom.'*

An ambulance man came up to Mick's Mum. 'We've got him out Mrs Farley. He's unconscious but alive. Would you like to go with him in the ambulance?'

She nodded and gave Mick's shoulder a squeeze. Then she moved forward to meet the stretcher.

I saw Mr Farley's face as they passed by. It was deathly white against the red blankets. The light on the roof began to flash and the siren wailed as the ambulance sped off.

The police put a big cordon around the whole area. Mick and I still stood staring at the scene of disaster. All was quiet now but the rain had started again.

As we turned to leave there was a movement in the trees beyond the landslide.

'There he is!' I said.

Mick saw him this time. The green man stood clear and solid except for his head.

I heard Mick gasp. I delved into my pocket and pulled out my camera, hoping it would work.

As I snapped the picture the green man was already beginning to disappear.

'Now do you believe me?' I asked.

'Yes,' whispered Mick. 'I didn't want to believe it before because if the green man was true, so was the curse.'

His voice ended in a sort of choke.

I'd never seen Mick look so scared. 'Come on, let's go home. Your Mum will ring from the hospital.'

We lay on our beds and fell asleep.

When we awoke Mum had good news.

'Your Dad's conscious,' she said, smiling. 'They say he has concussion and a broken leg but he'll be all right.'

Mick smiled and nodded. We got up and stood looking out of the window. What had caused the landslide? Had it really been the ancient curse?

It had been full moon, the underground waters were at their highest level and then there was all that rain. Also, the fact that the hillside there didn't have many trees to hold the soil together. We'd learnt about that in geography.

'I got a photo of him!' I said, remembering.

'Of my Dad?'

'No silly, of the green man.'

I turned to Mick. 'Do you think they'll still build there?'

He shrugged.

I decided it was worth a try. As soon as I could I had the film developed. If you looked hard you could see the green man although it was a bit hazy. I showed it to Mick's Dad when we went to visit him in hospital, and told him the whole story.

Mr Farley didn't exactly laugh but I got the impression that he wasn't convinced either. He studied the photo closely.

'Well, it does look a bit like the shape of a man,' he said, 'although it could just be shadows and foliage. Still, it's not me you need to see, it's the council. They gave me the contract.'

So Mick and I went to see the man in charge of building at the council offices. He too listened carefully to our story and looked at the photo. Then he shook his head.

'We won't be building there,' he said, 'but not because of any Forest Spirit or curse. That hillside is unstable and obviously subject to slides or flooding. What we're going to do is plant more trees.'

We looked at each other in triumph.

'You mean you're not going to build any houses or shops?' I asked.

'Oh yes, but not there. At the other end of the woods is an area of diseased trees.

They'll have to come down anyway. We're going to build there.'

So we had to be satisfied with that. We'd won in a way, or at least the green man had. I wondered if he would be satisfied. I knew he hadn't meant any harm to come to anyone. People had just got in the way. All he had wanted was to stop the trees from being cut down.

A few days later I went up to the spring to get Mum some more water for her eyes. It seemed to be working. She hadn't complained about them lately.

As I got near the pool I saw the green man sitting by the great oak.

His face was still a blur but I had the feeling that he was smiling.

Mum was smiling too, when I got home. And she was wearing a pair of glasses.

I stared, the bottle of water still in my hand.

'I needed glasses,' she said. 'That's what was causing the headaches.'

I put the bottle down on the table with a clonk. All that tramping up there for nothing! Still, it might be good for other things as well. I'd take some in for Mick's Dad. It might help his broken leg to mend.

THE END

Also available in the Reluctant Reader Series from:

PUBLISHING

Alien Teeth
Ian MacDonald

(Humorous Science Fiction)
ISBN 978 1 905637 32 2

Eyeball Soup
Ian MacDonald

(Science Fiction)
ISBN 978 1 904904 59 5

Chip McGraw
Ian MacDonald

(Cowboy Mystery)
ISBN 978 1 905637 08 9

Close Call
Sandra Glover

(Mystery - Interest age 12+)
ISBN 978 1 905 637 07 2

Beastly Things in the Barn   *(Humorous)*
Sandra Glover   ISBN 978 1 904904 96 0
www.sandraglover.co.uk

Cracking Up
Sandra Glover

(Humorous)
ISBN 978 1 904904 86 1

Deadline
Sandra Glover

(Adventure)
ISBN 978 1 904904 30 4

The Crash
Sandra Glover

(Mystery)
ISBN 978 1 905637 29 4

The Owlers
Stephanie Baudet

(Adventure)
ISBN 978 1 904904 87 8

Order online @ **www.eprint.co.uk**